SNOWMEN
ALL YEAR

Caralyn Buehner

pictures by
Mark Buehner

SCHOLASTIC INC.

Readers, see if you can find two ducks, a Tyrannosaurus Rex, a rabbit, a cat, and at least one hidden snowman in each painting.

ISBN 978-0-545-61326-2

Text copyright © 2010 by Caralyn Buehner.
Pictures copyright © 2010 by Mark Buehner.
All rights reserved. Published by Scholastic Inc.,
557 Broadway, New York, NY 10012,
by arrangement with Dial Books for Young Readers,
a division of Penguin Young Readers Group,
a member of Penguin Group (USA) Inc.
SCHOLASTIC and associated logos are trademarks
and/or registered trademarks of Scholastic Inc.

12 11 10 9 8 7 6 5 4 3 2 1   13 14 15 16 17 18/0

Printed in the U.S.A.   40

This edition first printing, September 2013

Designed by Lily Malcom
The art was prepared with oil paints over acrylics.

To Joyce and T

I love to build a snowman
On freezing winter days.
But when the sun is bright and warm
My snowman melts away.

There's nothing but a puddle
When my snowman disappears.
If only he were magic
And could stay with me all year!

I'd teach him how to fly a kite
High above the trees;

Then we would dig for pirate gold
Or sail the seven seas.

I know that he would love to see
The tigers at the zoo;

And at my birthday party
We would celebrate *his* too!

We'd go on all the wildest rides
At the amusement park,

But best of all would be the fireworks
Lighting up the dark.

On stormy evenings I would play
My favorite games with him;

On sunny days I'd teach him how
To dive and how to swim.

On summer evenings in the dark
We'd chase some fireflies,

Or sleep out in the quiet woods
Beneath the starry skies.

At the beach we'd play all day
(He'd get very sandy).

We'd trick-or-treat on Halloween
And bring home lots of candy.

Maybe this is magic snow
That will not disappear,

And this snowman will be the one
To stay with me all year!